Only the Best

GIRLS ONLY (GO!)

Dreams on Ice
Only the Best

GIRLS **2 GO** ONLY!

Only the Best

BEVERLY LEWIS

BETHANY HOUSE PUBLISHERS
MINNEAPOLIS, MINNESOTA 55438

Only the Best
Copyright © 1998
Beverly Lewis

Cover illustration by Paul Casale
Cover design by the Lookout Design Group

Published by Bethany House Publishers
A Ministry of Bethany Fellowship International
11300 Hampshire Avenue South
Minneapolis, Minnesota 55438
www.bethanyhouse.com

Printed in the United States of America by
Bethany Press International, Minneapolis, Minnesota 55438

Library of Congress Cataloging-in-Publication Data

CIP data applied for

ISBN 0–7642–2059–4   CIP

To

Alissa Jones,

a talented young gymnast
(and my cousin!)
who excels on the balance beam.

Author's Note

I would like to thank the International Federation of Gymnastics, the U.S. Olympic Committee, and Craig Bohnert, Public Relations Director at USA Gymnastics.

A special thank-you to Alissa Jones, a young gymnast with a bright future, and Amanda Hoffman, my cheerful "teen consultant." Smiles to Christy Friesen, who gave Jenna's cat the *purrr*fect name and personality to match!

Information about U.S. Olympic Gold medalist Dominique Moceanu was provided by her official homepage and her autobiography, *Dominique Moceanu, An American Champion.*

BEVERLY LEWIS is the bestselling author of over fifty books, including the popular CUL-DE-SAC KIDS and SUMMERHILL SECRETS series, and her adult fiction series, THE HERITAGE OF LANCASTER COUNTY. Her *Cows in the House* picture book is a rollicking Thai folktale for all ages. She and her husband have three children, as well as two snails, Fred and Fran, and make their home in Colorado, within miles of the Olympic Training Center, headquarters for the U.S. Olympic Committee.

CHAPTER 1

"You'll never guess who sent me a personal email last night," said Jenna Song as she opened her school locker.

Her best friend and locker partner, Olivia Hudson, scrunched her face into a silly frown. "Let me guess . . . someone famous?"

"Maybe."

"Someone like . . . Dominique Moceanu?"

Jenna spun around, her three-ring binder dangling from the top shelf. "That's it, Livvy! How'd you know?"

"You mean I'm *right*?" Livvy's green eyes sparkled. "I just guessed!"

Jenna rescued her sliding notebook with one hand and grabbed Livvy's arm with the other. "I'm so-o totally jazzed. See, I sent Dominique this really short email asking about her favorite gymnastics events and stuff like that."

"And she wrote you back?" Livvy asked.

"Domi adores the floor exercise and the balance beam. Just like me!"

"Domi?" Livvy eyed her curiously. "Sounds like you're on a first-name basis with one of the hottest gold medal gymnasts around."

Jenna shrugged. "Well, she signed off with her nickname—Domi. So . . . yeah, I guess I am!"

"Okay." Livvy looked a little suspicious.

Stepping aside, Jenna gave Livvy a chance to gather her books for morning classes. Their locker was major first-class—one of the coolest in Alpine Lake Middle School. At least Jenna thought so.

The top and bottom shelves were decorated in hot pink carpet, scraps left over from remodeling her attic bedroom. And with Christmas only five weeks away, they'd hung tiny green bows and gold bells on the door.

"So . . . when do I get a peek at your email?" Livvy asked, stacking up her books.

"Tonight after ballet class, maybe?"

"I'll have to check with my grandma first," Livvy said, looking a little worried. "She likes me to be prompt after ballet and skating sessions. 'It makes for a terribly late supper,' she always says."

"How's it going—her living with you and your dad?" Jenna leaned against the locker next to hers and Livvy's.

"As long as she doesn't pretend she's my mother, things are fine," Livvy said softly, closing the locker door. "Nobody can ever take Mom's place."

Jenna wished with all her heart that Livvy's mom had

somehow beaten the cancer last summer. More than any-thing!

"It's really not so bad having Grandma live with us," Livvy said. "For one thing, she's way better at cooking than Dad ever was."

They laughed about that, then discussed the possibility of Livvy actually going home with Jenna after ballet. "Mom can drive you to our house when she comes for me," Jenna offered.

Livvy fluffed her shoulder-length auburn hair. "Sounds super. Can't wait to read your email from . . . *Domi*!"

The girls giggled into their locker. No way did they want to be seen acting too silly. Even though they *were* on the sixth-grade end of the middle-grade totem pole!

But Jenna felt like flying. She was very excited about her personal connection with the youngest U.S. gymnast ever to win Olympic gold! She could hardly wait to tell Cassie Peterson, one of her teammates.

Jenna pranced to the end of the hall, jostled by the pre-homeroom crowd. "See you in P.E.," she called to Livvy as they parted ways.

"Okay!" Livvy waved and disappeared down the hall.

Jenna slowed her pace as she made the turn toward Mr. Lowell's homeroom. She'd rather be in any other class these days. Even strict Mrs. Smith—Livvy's homeroom teacher—would be light-years better.

Two annoying boys had started bugging her. Chris Ste-phens and Jamey Something-or-other were forever pulling on their eyes, making them slant down the way her eyes were shaped naturally.

"What kind of last name is *Song*?" Chris had jeered one day.

"Sing along with Jenna Song," Jamey Something had joined in.

Some days she could easily ignore them. But other times Jenna wanted to march across the room and tackle them good. She didn't want to risk hurting herself, though. Not *this* year! She was poised to move to a Level Nine in gymnastics. Nothing, especially not two terribly rude boys, was going to stand in her way!

After ballet class—and after Livvy had called home—the girls settled into Jenna's cozy attic bedroom. The room was cooler than cool with three large dormer windows on one side. On the opposite wall, her father had installed a barre and a wide mirror where she could practice her ballet moves and stretches. Sasha, her golden-haired cat, slept on the high four-poster bed, curled up in a tuck position. At the far end of the room, a built-in desk was home to Jenna's new computer. And high over the desk, an Olympic rings flag was tacked to the wall.

"Are you ready to preview my email?" Jenna said, sitting at her desk.

Livvy grinned and slid a chair next to her in front of the monitor. "Just think what fun we could've had with email when I lived back in Chicago."

"No kidding. As much as we *both* love to write letters, we probably would've been emailing nonstop." Jenna moved the mouse and clicked on the last entry. "Instead of pen pals, we could've been email amigos, right?"

"Yeah, and probably kissed your gymnastic goals good-bye . . . my skating plans, too," Livvy added.

"Never. Nothing comes between me and gymnastics." Jenna leaned forward. "Here we go . . . I found Dominique's message."

Livvy pressed in next to Jenna, studying the screen. "Wow, she says she can't live without her personal computer."

Jenna scrolled farther down. "Check it out—Domi collects lots of stuffed animals. Especially elephants. And guardian angels, too."

"Super," whispered Livvy. "Can you believe she told you all this stuff about herself?"

"I know. It's one of the coolest things to happen this year . . . next to you and me moving to the same Colorado town," Jenna said.

Livvy grinned at her. "You can say that again."

They abandoned the computer after a while, practicing their *arabesque* and *pirouette* moves together. "It's great having you in ballet class with me," Jenna said, catching her breath.

"For a while I wasn't sure if Dad was going to sign me up or not," Livvy said. "But thanks to Grandma, I'm in!"

Just then the computer announced an incoming email. Quickly, Jenna rushed back to her desk. She clicked the mouse to access the message. Scanning the screen, she read the words silently. "Oh, this can't be," she groaned, noting the name of the Denver adoption agency.

"Something wrong?" Livvy asked, coming over.

"Listen to this." She read the message aloud. " 'Friday, November 20. To Reverend and Mrs. Song: A healthy Korean infant is available for adoption. A certified letter with pertinent information will be sent to you immediately. Congratulations, and thank you for your patience in this matter.' "

Livvy turned to face Jenna. "Sounds like you're about to become a sister. How's it feel?"

Jenna's throat felt lumpy. "I didn't think it was going to happen so fast," she admitted, more to herself than to her friend.

Astonished, she went to sit in the soft, pillowed area under one of the dormer windows. Sasha came purring and made herself comfortable in Jenna's lap. Silently, Jenna stroked her cat's sleek coat.

"I don't get it. You seem upset," Livvy said, coming to sit on a floor pillow.

Reaching for her friend's hand, Jenna squeezed hard. "Oh, Livvy. I don't know how to say it, but I don't think I'm ready for this."

CHAPTER 2

First thing Saturday morning, Jenna headed for the gym—Alpine Aerials Gymnastics. AAG, for short. Padded safety mats were out everywhere when she arrived. Gymnasts in various levels practiced on the uneven parallel bars, balance beam, and the vault. Others worked individual floor routines. Graceful, fit bodies were flying, swinging, or tumbling all over.

Cool stuff, she thought. The gym was pure heaven on earth.

For as long as Jenna could remember, she had been testing her balancing ability on the narrow curbs in her neighborhood. Or on the lines of a checkered kitchen floor. As a preschooler, she'd posed on a step stool in front of the TV, pretending to be an Olympic medalist. And in her imagination, the crowd was always cheering. For her!

When she was three, her mother had enrolled her in a preschool gymnastics group called Tumble Tots. Jenna caught on quickly, and by the time she was in kindergarten, she was showing other tiny gymnasts how to tuck their knees for a forward or backward somersault. "Teacher's little helper," her coaches used to say.

She was still the shortest girl on her team. But Jenna didn't mind being petite. The closer a gymnast was to the ground, the better advantage in overall performance. At eleven, she was more than confident with her moves. Stunts like the back handspring, walkover, and the straddle split. She could perform her entire floor, vault, and balance beam routines without help from Coach Kim or his Russian-born wife, Tasya.

Today she focused her attention on a long, hard workout. In two short weeks, the eight-member All-Around Team would compete in downtown Colorado Springs—at the Olympic Training Center!

"Think we're ready?" she asked Cassie as they changed clothes in the locker room.

"We have to iron the small things," the tall, slender girl said, grinning with thumbs up.

"Right!" But Jenna wasn't so sure. She couldn't concentrate today. Her thoughts were on the baby who was coming to upset her house. Would she get her required sleep? Or would the baby howl and fuss all night? Babies made lots of racket, she knew. Her aunt and uncle had just had a new baby. Most of the time they looked wiped out. Being sleep deprived was *not* an option for a gymnast!

Worried, Jenna taped her hands, then began her stretching exercises and aerobics with the team. After forty minutes, her muscles felt pliable, like warm honey. She started work on her individual routine, aware of the soft-crash pads beneath her bare feet. Waiting for the musical cue, she practiced her salute for the judge, who today happened to be her coach, Benjamin Kim.

"Push . . . push to perfection," Coach Kim called, his hands high in the air.

Jenna focused her attention on her tumbling moves, especially the salto, front pike somersault, and aerial walkover. "Okay, time to show your stuff," she whispered to herself.

Impatiently, she bounced on her toes, anxious to start. She waited . . . and waited. But she heard no music floating through the speakers. Coach went to investigate.

While she waited, Jenna performed several back walkovers. All the while, she thought of the startling email. The one from the Denver adoption agency. The one that might change the outcome of her entire gymnastics future!

She'd made an attempt to talk to her parents last night—after Livvy Hudson left. But by the time Jenna printed out the important email, her dad was already busy with Sunday sermon notes. And her mother was talking on the phone to a sick church member.

Jenna had gone to bed without saying a word to either of them. As long as it was her secret, maybe it might not happen, she reasoned. Feeling terribly left out, she'd tried to tell God about her worries but didn't get very far before falling into a nightmarish sleep.

Now, as she anticipated the jazz melody to her floor routine, she knew she couldn't put off talking to her parents. She'd go right home and tell them about the baby. If she waited too long, the certified letter would arrive anyway. It was do or die!

Finally the musical selection began with the smooth, clear sound of the saxophone. Though Jenna had practiced the routine hundreds of times, she hesitated at the take-off point, arms out, chin up, toes pointed.

"You can do it, Jen!" shouted Coach Kim from the outside edge of the mat.

"We're rooting for you!" her teammates cheered and clapped.

"Go, girl!" shouted Cassie.

But hard as she tried, Jenna froze up on her tumbling pass and didn't go far enough on her somi-and-a-half. Her back handsprings were sloppy, and she tilted the landing on her aerial cartwheel.

All Jenna wanted to do was cry.

CHAPTER 3

Jenna confessed to her parents about the information she'd kept secret. "An email for Dad came through from the adoption agency," she said at supper, glancing at each of them. "You're getting a baby . . . very soon."

Her mother's eyes were wide with delight. And when she tried to talk, she nearly blubbered. "Oh, we had no idea . . . no idea at all that something would happen this quickly. My goodness! What wonderful news!"

Yeah, wonderful, thought Jenna.

Her father spoke up. "The caseworker told us we were in for a fairly long wait. So far, it's only been ten months since the initial application was approved."

"I'll call the agency first thing Monday," her mom added quickly. "They'll tell us if the baby is a boy or girl."

"We requested a *boy*," Dad spoke up. His face was actually glowing, like it was Christmas Eve or something.

Jenna couldn't stand it any longer. She stared down at

her plate, a lump growing in her throat.

"What's wrong, honey?" asked her mother. "Are you all right?"

She could hardly speak. "I . . . I thought you were happy with just me." Her words came out all squeaky.

"Oh, honey, we *are* . . . we're very happy." Dad reached across the table for her hand. "Mom and I have plenty of love to go around . . . enough for the new baby, too. We talked this over with you and the caseworker months ago. Remember?"

Jenna held in the sobs that threatened to burst out. Months ago? Back then she figured adopting a baby was probably years away for them. Maybe even never.

Dad continued. "And about using your computer . . . well, I knew you wouldn't mind. It was a handy way to keep in touch with our caseworker now and then," he said almost apologetically.

She nodded. Borrowing her computer wasn't the problem.

"We love you dearly, Jenna. And your mother and I want to give an orphaned child a chance. Make a difference somehow."

His words made Jenna feel even worse. "What about gymnastics and ballet? What will happen with that?" She couldn't continue. If she did, she might cry. And that would mean she was a selfish little brat. She certainly didn't want her parents to think *that* of her!

"Life will go on, same as always," Dad said, refolding his napkin. "You'll still attend gymnastics and ballet and school and church."

She hoped he was right, but it was hard to believe. Everything was going to change. She was sure of it!

Mom got up to clear the table. "We'll all travel together to greet our new baby," she said, looking suddenly younger than her years.

All of us?

"When?" Jenna asked.

"The certified letter will surely tell us," Dad said. He sat tall at the head of the table, his regular place. But tonight he looked more handsome than usual. His black hair shone in the soft luster of the dining room chandelier. His face was determined but compassionate.

Mom reread the email printout. "Sounds like we'll be hearing any day now."

Jenna wouldn't hold her breath for it. As long as the letter hadn't arrived, she could focus on the gymnastics meet. And something else, too. She had a feeling Coach Kim was going to make her captain of the team.

"I wish you would've told me we might be getting a baby this year," she said at last. "It's hard to think of someone that tiny . . . and noisy fitting in around here. With the three of us."

Mom placed a dessert dish of peach cobbler on the table. "Adopting a baby will take some getting used to," she said.

Dad smiled. "But we're willing to do whatever it takes to welcome a precious homeless child into our hearts."

Mom sat down and began dishing up the dessert. Her eyes twinkled with anticipation, and Jenna couldn't remember ever seeing her this excited.

"I can hardly believe it," Mom said. "We're going to have

a brand-new baby in the house. Very soon!"

"Yes, and we're going to give him or her lots of love," Dad said, accepting a generous serving of cobbler with a smile.

Jenna listened, staring at her dessert. They could go right ahead and shower plenty of love on their new baby, she decided. But what about *her*? Would they forget about their firstborn and her gymnastic goals?

Sunday afternoon, Jenna sat cross-legged on her bed and picked up the telephone. She punched the buttons to call Livvy.

"Hudson residence" came the delicate voice of Livvy's grandmother.

"Oh, hi," she said. "May I speak to Livvy, please? This is Jenna Song."

"Just one moment."

When Livvy answered, Jenna told her the latest. "My parents are so thrilled about the baby. They're dying to get some more details. Mom's calling the agency tomorrow."

"So they really *are* adopting a baby," Livvy said cheerfully. "Congratulations."

"Yeah, well, guess again."

"What's *that* supposed to mean?" asked Livvy. "Are you really that upset about it?"

Jenna clammed up. A long pause followed.

"Well?" Livvy was pushing. "Are you gonna talk to me or not?"

Sighing, Jenna asked, "Whose side are you on?"

"What are you talking about?" Livvy sounded puzzled. "Do you really think I'm against you?"

"You mean you aren't?"

" 'Course not," Livvy said. "I just think you sound, uh, insanely jealous."

She felt hideous. Livvy had no right! "Look, this conversation's going nowhere," Jenna said, the anger creeping into her cheeks.

"Well, you called *me*," Livvy replied. "So I guess you have the right to hang up whenever you want."

"Oh, is *that* how you feel?"

Click!

Jenna hung up on her friend. She dropped the receiver back into the cradle and just stared at it. "What's wrong with me?" she whispered, fighting back tears.

Livvy would be terribly hurt. She didn't deserve this sort of treatment. Not after losing her mom to cancer and having to move away from her Chicago hometown all in the space of a few months. Not after just moving here to Alpine Lake, Colorado—same as Jenna's family.

"Ohhh!" she groaned, lying there in her pajamas. "My whole life is falling apart!"

She could see it now. Her mom would want to rush out and start shopping for baby things. Years ago, they'd given away Jenna's old crib and high chair, so they were starting over from scratch. Starting over in more ways than one!

And there was the nursery. Her parents would expect her

to help them fix up the old guest room—turn the small room into something special.

On top of everything else, there probably wouldn't be time for anyone to drive her to gymnastics anymore. Mom would be too busy planning and preparing for the blessed baby event.

She sighed, worrying over every possible detail. *Once the baby arrives, what then?* she wondered.

Jenna skipped reading her Bible and her devotional book. She didn't bother to pray even the shortest prayer. Crawling into bed, she curled up in a ball. Hot tears slid down her face and onto the pillow. "Why me?" she cried. "Why *now*?"

CHAPTER 5

"Our big day is Saturday, December fifth," Jenna's mother announced at breakfast two days later. She held the certified letter in her hand.

Jenna felt her heart thumping hard. "December fifth? No way!" she said, her spoon in midair.

"What do you mean?" Dad said, looking aghast.

"That's the day of my gymnastics meet at the Olympic Training Center," Jenna blurted.

Dad was silent, and Mom was beginning to look mortified. "We'll just have to work something out," she said.

"No! I can't skip this event, Mom!" Jenna insisted. "I've been working forever to compete with the team."

Her mother nodded, brushing a loose strand of hair from her face. "I didn't mean that you'd have to miss the meet. Of course we want you to attend . . . and to do your very best."

Jenna had always been one to overlook things, including

conflict with friends at school and church. She had a way of just wanting to forgive and forget. But today she struggled with her stressful feelings and felt physically sick.

Excusing herself, she scooted away from the kitchen table. She trembled as she leaned against the archway to the dining room, unable to speak.

Dad's voice filled the awkward silence. "Jenna, dear, no other child can possibly change our love for you, if that's what's troubling you."

She felt tiny and weak, wishing he'd stop talking about how much they loved her.

"We've been asking God for another child for a long, long time," he was saying. "We wanted to adopt a Korean baby boy . . . to match our nationality."

Jenna spun around. "So . . . what you really want is a *son*?"

"Only because we already have a wonderful daughter!" His eyes were gentle, his face solemn. "We hoped you'd be as delighted as we are."

She voiced what she was thinking. "Just so this kid won't intrude on my life," she muttered.

But her mother had heard the cutting remark, and her look was stern. "What a selfish thing to say, Jenna."

Mom's right, she thought. *But I can't ignore the way I feel*.

"Hey, turtle eyes," Jamey Something whispered in homeroom.

Jenna looked the other way. She refused to give him the time of day.

"Yo, Swan Song," sneered Chris Stephens.

Get a life, she thought. One way to keep from losing her cool was to dream up a put-down in her head. She was the Queen of silent put-downs. And getting better at it every day!

During math period, Chris sat directly behind her. He kept whispering to her when the teacher wasn't looking. "Olive face," he taunted.

Her hair prickled on the back of her neck. Her father would say to ignore the boy. Better yet, turn the other cheek—the Bible way.

"Almond eyes," he scoffed.

She took a deep breath. In her imagination, she turned around and slapped him silly. Somehow, just thinking that way really helped. It was the same way she was able to focus on her gymnastic moves. Think it through, *see it*, then make it happen.

The only difference between imagining that she'd bopped the jerk a good one and actually doing it was the leftover feeling of frustration. And knowing it was the *wrong* thing to do—imagination or not.

Had she laid into him for real, he might never make fun of her again. And she'd feel better . . . maybe. But hitting him was not her style. Still, it was all Jenna could do to keep her attention on the math assignment.

When the teacher called on Chris, she had to stifle a laugh. *He's toast now*, she thought, watching him drag his feet to the chalkboard. Anybody could see he wasn't prepared. Probably hadn't even done his homework. Probably hadn't for a long time.

Secretly, she was glad. Maybe now he'd back off and give her some peace. Till English class, anyway.

She wished Livvy was in more of her classes. But two out of seven was better than none. She wondered how Livvy would act toward her today. Yesterday she had been thoroughly ticked off—didn't even eat lunch with Jenna. Didn't hang around the locker much, either.

Jenna couldn't blame her friend. After all, it was Jenna's own fault for hanging up.

Would Livvy ever forgive her?

During P.E., Jenna tried to strike up a conversation with Livvy. But Livvy didn't seem too interested in hearing about Chris and Jamey and their racist remarks. She kept leaning into her gym locker, away from Jenna.

"Did you hear anything I just said?" Jenna demanded. "Do you even know who I'm talking about?"

Livvy cast a painful look her way. "Oh, so *today* you're talking to me?"

Jenna nodded. "I know you're probably furious about the other night, and I don't blame you."

Livvy slammed her P.E. locker. "What was wrong with you, anyhow? You seemed so . . . so out of it. So angry."

"Yeah, I was." She didn't want to get into it. Not here in the middle of gossip city. "I'm sorry, Livvy. Can we talk later?"

Livvy stared at her feet, then slowly nodded. "I'll save a table at lunch," she said without looking up.

"Thanks, Livvy. I'll see ya." She hurried back to her own locker to towel dry her hair, thankful that she'd had it cut chin length before school started this year. Waist-length hair had become a major problem with all the extra hours at the gym.

Quickly, she pulled on her jeans and a soft blue sweater for her next class—science. Unfortunately, Chris and Jamey were in the class, too! She tried not to think about their insults. But she was more upset than she wanted to admit.

After brushing her damp hair, she hurried off to science just as the bell rang. The best part about showing up nearly late was getting to sit at the back of the classroom—far removed from the likes of Chris and Jamey.

She got seated at the desk and took out her folder. When she settled back to look at the teacher, the boys did that ridiculous slanty thing with their eyes. Two girls behind them poked them good, and they turned around.

Jenna congratulated herself on arriving almost late to science. Maybe she should do that in every class from now on. For the rest of the year!

She listened to every word Mr. Rahn was saying. All about plant phyla—species—and boring stuff like that. She doodled on a clean sheet of paper, mostly drawing symbols for the different gymnastic elements. Like the double salto forward—two loops moving to the right.

When the teacher called on her, she hadn't exactly heard what he'd asked. "I'm sorry," she sputtered. "Can you repeat the question?"

"Please see me after class, Jenna."

Her heart sank. She couldn't afford to get herself in

trouble at school. She'd always gotten pretty good grades—high *B*s and some *A*s—all through grade school. And now this year, too.

When the bell rang, Chris and Jamey walked past her desk and whispered, "Sing a sad, sad song, Jenna Song."

"Stay away from me," she said not so softly.

They kept strutting by, pretending they hadn't heard.

When everyone had cleared out of the room, Mr. Rahn motioned for her to come to his desk. "May I see your class notes?" he asked.

She swallowed hard. "My notes?"

He nodded, standing behind his desk. "You were taking some during class, weren't you?"

She was caught. "Uh, no, I wasn't, Mr. Rahn. But I *was* listening."

"Very well, but next time, it might be a good idea to sit closer to the front," he pointed out. "It seems you were a bit distracted today."

There was a good reason for that. And she almost told him about Chris and Jamey's constant insults. She was that close to blowing the whistle on them when in walked Livvy Hudson.

"Oh, sorry," Livvy said when she saw her friend and the science teacher talking.

"No . . . no," said Mr. Rahn. "Come on in, Livvy."

Her face turned instantly white. "I didn't mean to interrupt."

"We're almost finished here," the teacher replied. Then he turned back to Jenna. "Is it possible you're preoccupied with news of the baby . . . the one your parents are hoping to adopt?"

His question took her off guard. How could he possibly know?

"I . . . I don't understand," she muttered.

Mr. Rahn was actually looking like a proud father himself. "Well, if you ask me, I think it's terrific," he said, his arms folded across his chest. "Your dad and I keep running into each other at the library. Both of us are doing research on different things, of course. But we got to talking about your parents' plans to adopt a Korean baby. It's something my wife and I have discussed for years."

"Oh" was all Jenna could say. How many other people knew about the adoption?

The bell rang for lunch, and Mr. Rahn waved Jenna and Livvy out the door.

"Wow, that was weird," she told Livvy when they arrived at their locker.

"What was?"

"Mr. Rahn made me stay after class so he could tell me he knows about my parents' plan to adopt a baby."

"That *is* weird," said Livvy, piling her books into the lower section of their locker.

"I came that close to telling him about Chris and Jamey," Jenna said, lowering her voice.

"Why didn't you?" Livvy popped up to check her hair in the mirror attached to the locker door.

"If they keep it up, I'm going to the principal. Mr. Seeley can handle them," she said. "But don't tell anyone. I don't want it to get around."

"Like the news of the baby your parents want to adopt?" Livvy piped up.

Jenna shrugged. She couldn't deal with any of this. Not here, not now, and not with her best friend!

The whole idea bugged her—especially the possibility of having to miss out on the gymnastics meet. She *had* to attend the event in Colorado Springs. There was just no way she'd let an alternate gymnast take her place! Not so she could go off to some child-placement agency. Not for *anything* linked to a baby brother!

Jenna wasn't surprised when Tasya asked her to work in front of the mirrors. She scurried over to the far end of the gym. "I'm not smiling today . . . right?" she said.

"You are not smiling, yes," replied Tasya. "Why do you look completely miserable?"

Because I am, she thought.

"Things are not all right with you?" asked Tasya, who wore a white shorts set and a concerned frown.

Jenna shrugged. She wouldn't lie. "Let's put it this way—my life's never been so messed up."

"Well, we cannot have that." Tasya squatted on the floor next to her. "Do you want to tell me about the mess?"

"Not really, but thanks," she said, turning and forcing a fake grin at the mirror. "I'll get over it."

If I can, she thought.

"Well, remember, if you do need someone to talk with, I'm here . . . Coach Kim, too."

"Thanks. That means a lot." Jenna turned and finished her stretches at the barre. As best as she could, she centered her thoughts on the work at hand. The attitude of a gymnast had a lot to do with getting high marks. She knew she'd have to work very hard at pulling up her confidence level. It was important not to crumble under the pressure of the upcoming meet.

Cassie and two other teammates worked the uneven parallel bars at the other end of the gym with Coach Kim. Jenna headed toward them, watching Lara Swenson, the youngest girl on the team. Lara's dismount was a perfect twist and clean stick. Not the slightest bobble.

She breathed deeply, wondering how *she* would do today.

Coach called to her, "Jenna, come! Let's work your floor routine first thing." He motioned her over to the large floor mat. "I want you to focus on composition today—each individual skill is a building block. Remember that. Let's start with your tumbling pass."

She felt like a beginner all over again. It was so humiliating. Especially in front of her teammates, some younger and more advanced. "My aerial cartwheel was lousy last time," she admitted, taking her artistic stance at the edge of the mat.

"Now . . . Jenna, you must focus on what you came here to do," he stated. "And never, never give in to distraction. Push . . . push for perfection!"

Push for perfection. One of his favorite expressions.

She pushed, all right, hard as she could. Focusing, pointing, twisting, rolling, tucking, springing . . . flying through her routine. But on the aerial cartwheel, she lost her momentum and landed poorly.

Again and again she worked the move, always off on either her timing, height, or landing. Frustrated and concerned about her status on the team, Jenna was given a time-out.

Coach Kim strolled over to her at the drinking fountain. "Something's not working for you, Jenna," he said softly.

She couldn't deny it. "I'm freaking out."

"I can see that."

Still, she held back, not telling the reason for her frustration and lack of concentration. She recited aloud the key words to her floor routine just as Coach Kim had taught her and his girls to do. "Pose, speed, leap, twist, pike, double back."

When her ten-minute break was up, her coach led her to the vault area instead of the floor mat. "A change of apparatus might do you good," he said with an encouraging smile. "Just enjoy yourself, Jenna. Can you do that for me?"

She nodded. "I'll give it my best shot."

"That-a girl!"

Gripping her hands together, she stood at the end of the mat. She made a mental note of the masking tape mark on the floor, the springboard, and the horse beyond.

"Just have fun," she said to herself and ran hard down the runway. But her feet overshot the springboard by a fraction of an inch. Hardly any bounce. She toppled clumsily onto the soft pile of safety mats. So much for the first vault.

"Try again," Coach Kim called to her.

The second attempt was even worse. She didn't have enough speed, and the bounce wasn't high enough. A limp front handspring on the vault led to an imperfect stick, not straight and clean with both feet firmly planted on the mat.

Discouraged after practice, Jenna hurried home to shower and change clothes for supper. Her mother was picky about her coming to the table all sweaty or wearing a leotard. Jenna wondered what it would be like to have a laid-back mom. From the time she'd started gymnastics, Mom had expected only the best from her. Nothing less.

"If it's not worth doing one-hundred-and-ten percent, it's not worth doing at all," her mother would often say.

Only the best . . .

Jenna had adopted that standard for her life—ballet and gymnastics, especially. And Coach Kim and Tasya definitely promoted the vigorous approach. She wondered if they were thinking of dropping her from the team. After today's pitiful workout, she wouldn't be surprised.

"How was practice today?" her father asked as they were seated in the dining room.

"Pathetic." She fingered the lace table covering and stared at the cloth napkin under both forks.

"Well, tomorrow's another day," he replied. "Things will improve, you'll see."

Her mother carried a tray of serving dishes—rice, chicken, *kimchi*, and bean sprouts sautéed in sesame oil. "Did you tell Coach Kim and his wife about our baby?"

"Not yet." She thought of her science teacher but didn't offer to share the story. Jenna wasn't up to being scolded for doodling in class.

"Your father and I have discussed the upcoming meet," Mom said, still standing near her chair. "You've never missed a single competition, Jenna. Not even for illness." She sighed. "Not since your preschool classes began years ago."

Jenna knew what was coming. "But, Mom—"

"Just listen, please, Jenna," her father cut in.

Mom continued. "Even though it isn't a good idea to cancel so close to competition, we feel you can miss, just this once."

"I told you how I feel!" Jenna blurted. "I won't skip out on the team . . . just so you can go off and adopt somebody's baby!"

"Jenna Lynn Song!" Her father stood up. His napkin fell to the floor. "That is quite enough."

She felt the stain of shame on her face. But nothing more was said about her outburst or her poor posture at the table. She picked at the soggy rice and the garlic-flavored kimchi.

When will Mom start cooking like an American? she wondered, overflowing with anger.

After supper, Jenna slipped away to her room with Sasha, who seemed *purrr*fectly delighted to see her. "Hello, prissy kitty," she said, burying her face in the soft, golden coat. "I missed my sassy girl today."

Mew.

Sasha wasn't one for being fussed over. She liked to be petted and stroked, sure. But all this cooing and baby talk, well, enough already!

"Wanna help me write in my diary?" Jenna kissed her cat on the top of her soft head. "Do you?"

The cat blinked her eyes, uncaring.

"You curl up here, and I'll write." She positioned the cat in her lap, but Sasha didn't stay put. She bounded down off Jenna's lap and over to the bed.

"Okay, be that way." Unlocking her secret diary, Jenna was ready to record the events of her disastrous day.

Tuesday, November 24
Dear Diary,

Thanksgiving is only two days away. But I don't feel very thankful this year. My parents can't understand why I don't care about getting a baby brother. I guess they have no clue. Things are perfectly fine the way they are . . . just the three of us.

On top of everything else, I'm having trouble with my aerial cartwheel, something I've never flubbed before—not since I first learned how. It's gotta be the baby thing. I just can't concentrate very well! But I won't give up, and I won't let Coach Kim and Tasya down.

What am I going to do?

CHAPTER 8

Thanksgiving Day was filled up with relatives and friends at her father's Korean church. The coolest thing to happen was Livvy's arrival, just in time for supper. The girls sat with other teenagers, eating noodles and kimchi leftovers, talking and laughing together.

Jenna introduced Livvy to her Korean pals as her "best all-American friend. She's an incredible figure skater . . . headed for the Olympics."

"Someday," whispered Livvy, tugging on Jenna's shirt.

"Yes, *someday* we'll watch her on TV and say 'we knew her when.'" She turned to Livvy. "Are you totally embarrassed yet?"

Livvy's face was growing redder by the second. "Did you have to say all that?"

"Don't be ashamed of your skating talent, girl. God gave it to you for a reason," Jenna said.

"I'm not ashamed. Just modest, I guess."

"That's cool. So . . . *I'll* brag on you," Jenna said, laughing.

When the dishes were cleared away, the group games began. The kids and the grown-ups played for more than an hour.

Darkness soon settled over Alpine Lake, and church members began offering testimonies of thanksgiving.

Jenna's uncle Nam, a new father, stood tall and held up his tiny son. "We are very grateful to God for a healthy child this year," he said, grinning.

Another man stood and thanked the church for helping him through hard times. His wife stood at his side, smiling and nodding, giving thanks in Korean.

Next, Jenna's mother stood and told everyone about the baby they were going to adopt. From that moment on, Pastor Song's soon-to-be-adopted son was the topic of conversation. Talk of a baby shower hummed in the air, and the church ladies chattered in Korean, smiling and planning.

Oh great, thought Jenna. She was sure she'd have to attend all the hoopla for her adopted brother. The whole thing was getting out of hand!

A light snow was falling as Jenna and her friend headed for the church parking lot. She was glad she'd worn her warmest jacket and scarf. Winter in the Colorado Rockies meant skiing, snowboarding, and other exciting activities. Best of all for her was working out in a heated gym!

On the way to the car, Livvy commented, "Your church

is really super. So friendly and connected, like a community."

"Asian-Americans stick together. And one of the best things about going to a Korean church is getting to hear the sermons in my first language."

"Thanks for inviting me. I like the unique culture—especially the noodles." Livvy pulled on her mittens. "I'll have to get your mom's recipe. They're super good."

"Nothing to it," explained Jenna. "Just tell your grandma to sauté them in sesame oil. It gives that yummy flavor."

The girls waited beside the Songs' family car. "Do you ever speak Korean around the house—you know, with your parents?" asked Livvy, leaning against the car door.

"Lots of times. And even sometimes at gymnastics because my coach is Korean, too."

"And Tasya is Russian," Livvy added. "I wonder how that works out at their house?"

Jenna chuckled. "Their kids probably speak three different languages."

"Really? They have kids?"

Jenna honestly didn't know. She'd never heard either of them talk about children. Come to think of it, they probably didn't. Their "kids" were all the girls who trained at their gym.

Nothing more was said about the upcoming adoption. And Jenna was relieved. She'd heard more than enough talk of a new brother at church for one day.

CHAPTER 9

For as long as she could remember, Jenna had preferred home meets. Even though AAG was smaller than a big-city gym, it was easier doing routines on familiar apparatuses where she trained three times a week. And there were the usual ceiling marks she liked to watch when she did her aerials. The spots helped keep her position when she was in the air.

But all the girls on the team were jazzed about going to the Olympic Training Center headquarters. Especially Cassie Peterson, the tallest sixth grader. "I've heard all kinds of awesome stuff about OTC," she said, her blue eyes shining.

"Like what?" Jenna asked as they dressed in leotards in the locker room.

"For one thing, the equipment is state-of-the-art." Cassie seemed pretty sure of herself. "A first-class place."

"It oughta be."

"OTC oozes with excellence and professionalism," said Cassie, her face beaming. "I can't wait to go again."

"Me neither, except this'll be my *first* time."

"You'll love it, trust me." Cassie sighed, looking a bit discouraged. She looked almost sad.

"What's wrong?" Jenna asked.

"It's just that . . . oh, I'm not really sure about gymnastics anymore."

Jenna sat on the bench beside her. "What're you saying?"

Cassie straightened. "It's a good thing we're going, I guess. This'll probably be my last year at AAG," she said suddenly.

"You're kidding!" Jenna was shocked. "You've been involved with gymnastics since you were in preschool. I thought you were in this forever. Like me . . ."

"I thought so, too, but I just don't know anymore." Cassie pulled on her white warm-up pants, her gaze directed toward Jenna. "It's such a big commitment. You know what I'm talking about."

Jenna knew. She knew as well as anyone at AAG. To achieve Elite level—which had been both Cassie's and Jenna's dream—required an exhausting training schedule. Thirty hours a week, at least, just to maintain Elite status. And there were always injuries just waiting to happen. With that much pressure, a gymnast was often subject to broken bones, sprains, or worse.

She watched Cassie twist her long, blond locks into a knot at the back of her head. For a single moment, Jenna almost missed her own waist-length hair. Then she spoke up. "You won't quit without thinking it through, will you?"

Cassie closed the door to her locker. "That's just it. I've been thinking nonstop ever since the qualifying meet last spring. If I keep testing up—to Level Nine and finally to Elite level—I'll have to drop out of public school. Probably have to be homeschooled."

"So what's wrong with that?"

Cassie shrugged. "I really like going to regular school. Besides, my parents don't have time to school me at home."

Jenna didn't know what to say. She couldn't imagine Cassie quitting gymnastics. "I guess we'd better get going," said Jenna, removing her watch and earrings. Jewelry was not allowed during practice or competitive sessions. It was one of the many safety rules Coach Kim and Tasya insisted on for *every* gymnast.

"Coach'll wonder where we are," Cassie said with a sigh.

"Yeah, probably" was all Jenna said.

Cassie stayed behind in the locker room. "I'll see you later . . . at warm-ups."

"Better hurry," Jenna advised, rushing out of the locker room.

More than ever, she was determined to attend the meet in Colorado Springs. Not because Cassie was so up in the air about gymnastics. It wasn't that. Jenna just could never think of turning her back on the sport.

Lost in thought, she zoomed out the girls' locker room door.

Crrrunch!

She plowed straight into Coach Kim. "Oh, I'm sorry." Her hand flew out to steady him. "I didn't see you, Coach. Are you all right?"

He caught his balance and chuckled, towering over her. "I'm quite fine . . . but what about *you*, young lady?"

"A little startled, that's all." And she turned toward the hallway, leading to the gym. "See you at the balance beam."

"Jenna . . . wait," he called to her. "There's something I want to ask you."

She whirled around, wondering what was on his mind. "Yes?"

"I want you to be team captain for the rest of the school year. What do you say?" His face was very serious. He meant business.

"Sure, I'll do it."

He clapped his hands twice. "Done! Now, get going . . . lead the stretches today."

"You got it!"

He was smiling his big polar bear grin. "I'll be in for tumbling warm-ups."

"Okay, Coach. See ya!" She couldn't remember feeling so terrific. Coach Kim really believed in her, even though she'd had some trouble with her floor routine. He knew what kind of stuff Jenna Song was made of.

Head high and shoulders back, she hurried through the doors and into the gym.

Friday, November 27
Dear Diary,
It felt great not having school today—the day after

Thanksgiving. Mom and Dad hit the mall for the start of the Christmas shopping season—for baby furniture (what else!)—while I worked out at the gym.

Being team captain is so cool. I think it's actually going to help me with my routines. My aerial cartwheels are improving, too. Yes!

I wrote another email to Dominique Moceanu. Even if she never answers again, I'm thrilled about getting her first reply. If only I could perform under pressure the way SHE does! Wow!

Cassie's got me worried about our team. She's definitely losing interest . . . or something's happening. I wish I knew what to do to help. Maybe I'll give her a call on the weekend. Maybe I'll pray for her, too.

CHAPTER 10

"I'm so glad it's almost Christmas," Jenna said, steadying the tabletop Christmas tree in the waiting area at Alpine Aerials Gymnastics.

"Me too," said Lara Swenson, the youngest girl on their team. "What're you getting this year?"

"I haven't asked for anything," Jenna said, bending each artificial branch carefully. "What do *you* want for Christmas?"

"A new warm-up suit and a bigger gym bag would be great," Lara spoke up.

She glanced at the petite girl. "A new water bottle might fit in my stocking." She laughed.

"That's *all* you want?" Lara's big brown eyes got even bigger.

"Well . . . maybe I'll ask for another Olympic rings flag for my room. I already have the small one." She couldn't honestly think of anything she needed or wanted. Unless it was some new church clothes. Her parents had already forked out a lot of money for her birthday present at the end of the summer—a classy new computer. Besides, she figured most of her dad's salary would go toward the new baby.

One by one, Jenna hung little wooden ornaments on the tree. The decorations were tiny gymnastics apparatuses or figurines of boys and girls performing various stunts. She and Lara had volunteered to decorate the tree yesterday when Tasya mentioned it after class. Jenna had jumped right up, saying she'd help. Anything to get her mind off the upcoming adoption. But she hadn't told Tasya the reason for her eagerness. Not Lara, either. So far, no one at the gym knew about the baby.

"Oh, look . . . how clever!" Lara had discovered a garland of wooden beads mixed in with Olympic rings and flags.

"Hey, cool," Jenna said, inspecting it. "I wonder where Tasya found this."

"They travel all over the world," Lara said, winding the garland around the tree. "Could've come from almost any-where."

"Looks like something from Germany." Jenna had seen similar holiday trimmings in the catalogs that sometimes arrived in the mailbox. "There's only one way to know," she observed.

"Ask Tasya, right?" Lara giggled as she spun around the room, pointing her toes and posing.

Jenna stepped back and examined the tree. "So . . . what do you think?" she asked. "Are we good at this or what?"

"Oops, I see an empty spot." Lara rushed over to fill it with two additional ornaments. "There, how's that?"

"The best," Jenna said, studying the tree again.

Lara stood against the wall, staring at her. "You do everything that way, don't you?"

"What do you mean?"

"You never miss a chance for perfection." The younger girl wore a curious expression. "Am I right?"

Jenna had to laugh. "You didn't see my floor routine last Saturday, did you?"

Lara frowned. "You're kidding. You mean you actually flubbed?"

"Not only that, I wiped out!"

"I must've been working on bars," Lara said. "I totally missed it."

Jenna shook her head. "I'm surprised none of the girls said anything. I had an all-around lousy practice," she confessed.

"Well, I never heard about it."

Jenna wandered over to the vending machines, where only healthy foods were available. She selected a can of pure carrot juice. "That's one of the cool things about our team," she said, pulling the flap off the can. "We support each other."

"Like Coach always says—we're family around here. We work together." Lara selected an apple juice from the juice machine and a fruit yogurt from the snack machine. "Want some of this?"

"No, thanks. I better work out a little before I go home," she said, glancing at her watch. "I'll see you later, Lara."

"Thanks for helping with the tree."

"We'll do it again next year, okay?" Jenna called over her shoulder.

Anxious to work on the uneven bars, she hurried to the locker room, changed clothes, and got herself focused. Several other girls from the team were working their floor routines.

Jenna did all her warm-ups—running, sit-ups, jumps, and her drills. When she was ready, she asked Tasya to spot her.

Tasya came willingly, as always. "You seem happier, yes?"

Jenna nodded. "I'm trying."

"Good, then. Let's hit everything today."

Hitting everything was a gymnast's single goal. "I'll do my best." She placed grips over her palms and wrist supports. Next, she applied some chalk and water to keep her fingers from slipping on the bars. Saluting, she raised one arm over her head, even though there was no judge in sight. Not today, but very soon . . .

Jenna felt totally confident about this routine. Because she loved bars. Since the days of Tumble Tots, she had practiced her technique thousands of times. It took courage and confidence, above all.

Mounting the lower bar, she felt the smoothness beneath her grip. *Hit everything*.

Tasya backed away slowly. "Remember now, Jenna: Always, *always* focus on your body. Know precisely where you are up there," she told her. "You *know* just where your toes end and where your fingertips begin, yes? Feel . . . know . . . *own* the weight of your body."

Jenna began with a gentle swing up to a handstand on

the lower bar. *Smooth, stretch, pike, handstand, catch, back salto* . . . The key words for each second of her routine, combined with muscle memory, carried her through to the most difficult part of her bars routine. The Geinger. She released the bar and caught it again as she circled around in midair.

Big swing, stretch, twist, smooth, double swings . . . The dismount was a layout with a full twist. Her feet pounded the safety mat, jarring her body.

"Clean stick! Very good!" shouted Tasya, her face beaming.

Jenna couldn't help grinning as she threw her arms high over her head. There was no question in her mind. She had performed only her best.

She left the gym with one thought buzzing around in her head. *I have to work on a stronger floor routine . . . especially my aerial cartwheels!*

CHAPTER 11

At church the next day, Jenna bowed her head silently during prayer time. She prayed for Cassie and for herself—about the aerial cartwheels and the upcoming meet.

Jenna had no interest in doing the same for little Jonathan—the name her father had already chosen for the baby. If she *did* bring the matter up, God wouldn't understand her uncaring attitude.

After the sermon was given and the benediction sung, the women went to cook in the fellowship hall. Every Sunday they served up a feast. And every Sunday the church members—visitors, too—gathered downstairs and ate kimchi and noodles and other Korean specialties to their hearts' content.

This Sunday was no different, except that Jenna sat off by herself. Several young people tried to coax her to join them, but she refused. She was miserable, just like Tasya

Kim had said five days ago. Miserable and stuck with the pain of jealousy.

That afternoon, Jenna called Livvy from her portable bedroom phone. Livvy answered on the second ring. "Hi, it's me," Jenna said. "I'm glad you're home. I need some company. Can you come over?"

"I have a few more pages of homework, but maybe I can. Wait a minute, I'll ask my dad." Livvy wasn't gone for more than a few seconds. "Sure, my dad said he'll drive me over."

"Cool! I'll be waiting." She nuzzled her face against Sasha's furry body. "Bye!"

Jenna hung up and went to turn on her computer. When she checked her email, she was surprised to see another message from Domi . . . or probably someone representing the Dominique Moceanu Homepage. With thousands of messages pouring in, there was no way America's little sweetheart gymnast could possibly keep up. No way!

The email began: *Hi, Jenna! I hope you do well at your meet in Colorado Springs. You'll love OTC. It's a great place to "show your stuff." Have fun!*
Domi M.

Jenna hurried downstairs to tell her parents. But Mom was taking a nap, and Dad was brushing up on his notes for the evening vespers.

Sitting on the sofa, Jenna watched for Livvy. On the coffee table, she noticed a brochure of an adoption agency. She studied the front and discovered that it was the one her parents were working with.

Casually, she thumbed through the pages, surprised at how many children and infants were featured. Most of them had lived their short, needy lives in overseas orphanages. Without the love of a permanent family. Their tiny faces touched her, made her feel sorry for them. Each one.

Sighing, she wondered how she might've felt about an adopted brother if she hadn't spent the last nearly twelve years as an only child. *Would I care more about baby Jonathan then?*

She turned the pages more slowly, studying the ethnic children. Indian, Chinese, Korean, Filipino. Many of them had already been approved for adoption. They were just waiting for loving parents. So many children . . .

The doorbell startled her.

Quickly, she opened the front door to Livvy. "Come in," she said, greeting her friend. "Glad you came over. Want some pop or something?"

"Super." Livvy removed her jacket and wool hat. She wore a tan turtleneck and brown corduroy jeans. "It's starting to snow again," she said, shaking her hair a bit. "My dad said he'll pick me up in a couple of hours."

"That's good." Jenna hung up Livvy's coat and hat in the hall closet. Then she led her into the kitchen. "Wanna make root beer floats? Or are you too cold for ice cream?"

"Whatever you like." Livvy was perched on the edge of a chair.

Jenna laughed. "Hey, I think we've switched roles."

"Like how?"

"You're the relaxed one these days," she said, dipping ice cream into two tall glasses.

"So why're *you* uptight?" Livvy asked, leaning back in her chair. "You've got one of the best gymnastic coaches around, a fabulous ballet instructor, and two terrific parents."

Jenna noticed the obvious absence. Livvy hadn't said one word about Jonathan, the soon-to-be baby brother. "So you think I should be perfectly calm and relaxed? My world's totally together, right?"

Grinning, Livvy waved her hand. "Oh, whatever."

"Yeah, right. Whatever." Jenna set about pouring the root beer over the ice cream. It foamed up, threatening to spill over the sides.

"You've got everything a girl could possibly want," Livvy continued. Then she paused, staring out the window. "You know, I'd give almost anything to have my mom back. But that's selfish of me. I know that."

Selfish . . .

Jenna didn't want to touch that topic. She didn't need to feel guilty today, on top of everything else. "Your mom was always involved with your skating, wasn't she?" Jenna asked.

Livvy's eyes glistened suddenly, and she turned from the window. "Mom took me to every skating event from the time I was in preschool on. She went along to cheer for me, but she was never uptight about competitions. Not like some moms on the sidelines."

"Like *my* mom," Jenna said softly. She carried the root beer floats over to the table and sat down. "My mother is so strict . . . expects way too much. Especially in gymnastics."

"But that's a good thing, isn't it?" Livvy spoke up.

Jenna dipped a straw into her float. "It all depends, I guess."

"On what?"

She wasn't sure how to explain what she felt. "It's just that my mom wants me to achieve—keep pushing myself—because she knows I can reach my goals."

Livvy was nodding her head. "What's so bad about that?"

"She's stuck on me being the best."

"Lots of moms want that for their kids." Livvy was staring at her now.

Jenna shrugged, feeling almost sad. "But it sounds like your mom was different . . . didn't push so hard."

"Oh, she did, but in a gentle way. But best of all, my mom accepted me. That was always number one with her." Livvy leaned down to sip her soda.

Jenna thought it over. "That's the kind of mom I want to be someday. The ideal mom—someone like your mother."

"You know what I think?" Livvy said.

Jenna shrugged.

"Better be thankful for what you have," Livvy offered.

Jenna ignored the comment. She didn't need another sermon. That wasn't why she'd invited Livvy over. The truth was she felt lonely—needed a listening ear. She honestly wished she could talk to her own mother like this. But Mom was too busy arranging baby furniture and sewing nursery curtains to listen to the child she already had.

Monday, November 30
Dear Diary,

The meet at OTC is this Saturday! I talked to Cassie at school today, trying to get her psyched up for the event. But she seems so wiped out. Even after volleyball in P.E. I wonder if she's pushed herself for too long.

Will that happen to me? I really hope not because my goal to qualify for the Junior National Team someday is still VERY strong. If Cassie drops out at the end of the year, her decision might bring the rest of the team down (so to speak).

I wonder what Coach Kim and Tasya would say if they knew Cassie was struggling? Maybe they could help boost her spirits. . . .

Jenna finished writing her diary entry, then reached for the phone. She dialed Cassie's phone number. "Hey, Cass," she said when her friend answered. "Busy?"

"Doing homework. What's up?"

"I was wondering," she began. "Have you talked to Coach and Tasya about what you told me last week?"

Cassie gasped. "Are you kidding? They're professional coaches, Jenna. They'd never understand what I'm dealing with."

"I think you're wrong. Why not give them a try? They might help."

Cassie was silent.

"Look, I don't mean to get on your case, but I hate to see you feeling like this about gymnastics. Someday soon you and I are going to the qualifying meet for Elite gymnasts . . . aren't we?"

"Well, maybe."

"So you haven't decided for sure?" Jenna's fingers were crossed.

"I won't give up without a fight—my own personal battle, that is."

Jenna understood. "I know, Cassie, and I'm praying for you, okay?"

"That's probably a good thing." Cassie chuckled a little. "I need all the help I can get."

"Hang in there, girl," Jenna said, glad she'd called.

"Thanks, I will."

"See ya at practice tomorrow."

"Okay, bye."

Jenna hung up the phone. She leaned back on her bed, staring at the ceiling. Sasha came over and settled down next to her. "Something's really bugging Cassie," Jenna told her cat. "I hope she snaps out of it before Saturday."

Sasha's purring rose to a gentle roar. And Jenna closed her eyes and began to pray.

After supper, Jenna made herself cozy near the fireplace with Sasha in her lap. Dad sat on the sofa next to Mom as he read the Bible and the family devotional. Jenna stared into the orange and gold flames as she listened.

The reading was about changes and learning to trust God through them. She wondered if her father had searched the book just to find this topic. But she didn't shut out the message because of it. She didn't feel upset about the things her dad was reading. Not the way she might have a week ago.

Gazing into the fire, she remembered the images of orphaned babies and children from the agency pamphlet. She remembered how stirred up she'd felt the first time she'd seen it. Maybe because the pages represented the caseworkers that had located baby Jonathan for her parents. And for her. . . .

The longer she sat there, the worse she felt. In a few days, a baby was coming to Alpine Lake. *Her* parents would become *his*. And she would become Jonathan Song's big sister!

She knew she ought to be getting ready for the special day. But how?

CHAPTER 13

Jenna met Livvy at their locker first thing Tuesday. "How'd skating go this morning?" she asked.

"Really super," Livvy replied, carrying her skate bag over her green parka.

"That's the stuff!" Jenna put both thumbs up and waved them in Livvy's face. "You can brag on yourself once in a while, especially to your friends. How's it feel?"

Livvy laughed, depositing her jacket and the books for her afternoon classes inside the locker. "No comment," she said.

Jenna watched her stack up her math and English books. The little Christmas bells taped to the locker door jingled as the girls took turns primping at the mirror.

"I've been thinking about your gymnastics event—the one coming up," Livvy said, turning to face her. "I've got a brainwave about it."

Oh, great. Jenna braced herself. She had a feeling she

knew what Livvy was going to say. Something about traveling to Denver with her parents to bring the baby home. "Uh . . . if this is about skipping the meet, I can't do it." She closed the locker door so hard the tiny bells kept jingling inside.

"You mean you *won't* do it," Livvy shot back. "Anybody knows your coach'll let you off. That's what alternates are for."

"Livvy, stop!"

"Look, I'm not on your case, Jen. I just think you should change your mind."

Change . . .

There it was again.

Jenna stood her ground. "I'm not a horrible person, really. I just can't let my coach or the team down."

Livvy got right in her face. "Listen, I have an idea . . . but only if you really want to go with your parents to get your baby brother."

"It's not possible!" Jenna spun away on her heels, not wanting to hear more. She tore off toward homeroom. And to the face-making weirdoes, Chris and Jamey.

Sitting at her regular desk, she pulled her notebook out of her book bag. She found her assignment book and double-checked her homework. All the while, Chris and Jamey were yanking on their eyes.

Any other day, she might've overlooked them—put up with their antics one more time. But now she'd had enough.

Up! Her hand flew high.

Chris and Jamey blinked their eyes and jerked their heads at attention. They shuffled around in their desks, probably looking for a book . . . something to make them look busy.

Jenna held her hand even higher, hoping Mr. Lowell would hurry and look her way before she lost her nerve. She sat as tall as she could in her seat. Filled with confidence, she was reaching for the uneven parallel bars in her mind. She was doing her best to "see" her routine, while Mr. Lowell paid absolutely no attention.

Stretch, catch, swing, kick . . .

Mr. Lowell looked up. "Yes, Jenna?"

"Uh . . ." She glanced over at Chris and Jamey. Could she follow through?

Beat the nerves, Coach Kim was always saying.

She took a deep breath. "I need to see you after class, please," she said.

"That will be fine," her homeroom teacher said.

Chris and Jamey wilted like old lettuce. And they didn't look her way even once with a rude or racist gesture the entire period.

Despite her worries, things went okay with Mr. Lowell. "I'm glad you told me, Jenna. I won't tolerate that sort of behavior in my homeroom," he insisted when she'd spilled out the whole story.

"I really didn't want to get anyone in trouble," she was quick to say. "It's just that . . . well, I'm sick and tired of their faces and constant slurs."

"You shouldn't have to put up with that nonsense." He

smiled at her. "I'll handle things."

Before she left the classroom, he thanked her.

"I hope I did the right thing," she said.

"You did the *best* thing for Chris and Jamey. Mr. Seeley will want to know about this."

Mr. Seeley—her principal—would come down hard on the boys. She was sure of it.

Rounding the corner to math, she spied Chris and Jamey. Their drooping faces gave them away. "We don't like snitches," Chris said, mustering up some courage.

She kept walking, ignoring them.

"Why'd ya have to go and tell?" Jamey whined, following close behind her.

She stopped. "Why'd you have to keep bugging me?"

Their mouths dropped open.

"You've had your warped fun, now leave me alone!" With that, she turned and escaped into her math class.

Relieved to be in a class without the boys, she chose a desk close to the front. Taking a deep breath, she opened her homework.

Out flew the adoption pamphlet. "What's this doing here?" she whispered and leaned down to rescue it from the floor.

"Hey, what's that?" someone said.

Jenna sat up to see Cassie sliding into the desk across the aisle. "Oh, it's . . ." She almost said "nothing."

"Let's see it." And before Jenna could stop her, Cassie reached for the brochure.

Jenna's heart was pounding. She didn't want *everyone*

to know about her parents' plans for adoption. It wasn't anyone else's business!

"Where'd you get this?" Cassie persisted, turning the pages.

Jenna felt her face burning. "I . . . uh, can we talk about this later?"

Cassie glanced around. "How come?"

"Just because." Jenna's embarrassment was turning to anger.

"Is somebody in your family going to adopt a baby?" asked Cassie, leaning over and handing the pamphlet back.

Jenna didn't want to admit it. But she felt almost helpless, afraid of what Cassie might think. Especially if her friend knew how selfish Jenna had been.

Cassie crouched on the floor beside her. "Listen, Jenna, not too many people know this, but *I'm* adopted. And it's the greatest thing . . . really."

Surprised, Jenna looked—*really* looked—at her friend. "I never knew that."

"Well, it's true. Just ask my parents." Cassie's eyes sparkled with her smile.

"That's amazing."

"My big sister thought so, too, way back when," Cassie said as she looked inside her book bag. Out came her wallet, and the next thing Jenna saw was a snapshot of Cassie and her older sister. "Stacy's nearly ten years older, but that never kept us from being close."

"But . . . I thought Stacy was your *real* sister. She looks so much like you," Jenna managed to say.

"She's a real sis, all right. In every way that counts. And

about looking alike, well, my parents just happened to hook up with an agency that matched ethnic backgrounds."

"Cool," Jenna said. And she meant it. What Cassie had just said *was* really cool. In fact, the same thing was going to happen to her and her new baby brother.

In every way that counts...

Jenna couldn't get the words out of her head!

When the bell rang at the end of first hour, Jenna could hardly wait to find her best friend. What *did* Livvy have in mind for this Saturday?

Dashing back to their locker, she hoped to find Livvy there. No sign of her friend in the hall. She'd have to wait till P.E.

Frustrated, she trudged off to a gigantic English test. *How will I ever survive this day?* she wondered.

CHAPTER 14

There was no time to grab a conversation with Livvy during or after P.E. So Jenna headed off to gymnastics without hearing her best friend's plan.

Things actually went well with the team. All eight of them. Jenna led warm-ups—twelve long stretches and several tumbling passes for each girl.

Then Coach Kim came over and gave them a solid pep talk. He was known for his short but straight-to-the-point approach. His talks made his gymnasts think and remember long afterward.

"We're here to do our best," he said. "Only our best."

Jenna glanced at Cassie, sitting next to her on the bench. She wondered how the zip in Coach Kim's voice might affect Cassie's final decision.

Coach continued. "Are we a team? Are we in this together? Do we breathe, see, and taste victory?"

The girls nodded, some clapping after each question.

Jenna saw the enthusiasm on Coach's face and the energy in his step as he paced back and forth. His words made her feel as if she were born to do the sport. More than anything, she wanted to compete. More than anywhere else, she could be herself inside the walls of a gym. She was at home here. At Alpine Aerials Gymnastics!

And things would go just fine in Colorado Springs, too. She was sure of it. They were a team. Like family.

We're in this together....

On the drive home, Jenna kept sneaking glances at her mom. "You should've heard Coach Kim today," she said as they waited at a red light. "He was really pounding nails."

Her mother seemed dazed, out of it. "I'm sorry, what did you say, Jen?"

"Coach Kim . . ." She stopped. No sense repeating herself. Mom was in nursery land somewhere. Jenna knew by the dreamy look in her eyes. And even though Mom seemed to be paying attention to traffic, her mind was probably on Jonathan—a gift from God. That's what his name meant in the book of names Dad had purchased.

Jenna had sneaked a peek at the name book. She'd looked up the baby's name. Hers too. Jenna meant "God is gracious." Seeing those words after her name made her feel special.

"You must see the darling nursery lamp I bought today," Mom was saying.

Jenna was right. Her mom *was* daydreaming about the new baby.

"It's the cutest thing. A white sliver of a moon with a cow jumping over it." Mom pulled into the parking spot at the curb in front of their three-story brick house. "I almost bought the lamp with the Humpty Dumpty design on it, but there was just something wonderful about that cow. . . ."

Jenna didn't attempt a comment. Nothing she might've said or asked would have been heard or answered anyway. Honestly, she'd never seen her mother like this. Not even the day Jenna placed first at State on beams and bars two years ago!

"Let's head right upstairs," her mom said, pulling the parking brake. "I want to show you something."

Jenna got out on the street side and waited for her mother to come around. The sidewalk was slushy now from yesterday's snow. All day long, the sun had warmed things up, making the first day of December almost a no-jacket day.

"God's smiling down on us," Mom said as they walked up the steps to the house.

"You mean because of the mild weather?" Jenna thought she'd laugh but held it in. Mom wasn't her normal self. Not one bit!

Upstairs in the nursery, Jenna checked out the cow-jumping-over-the-moon lamp. It really *was* different. And cute. "I've never seen anything like this," she told her mom.

"Neither have I." Turning toward the closet, Mom went

in search of something. "I want you to have a look at this, Jenna," she said, her body halfway into the closet.

Jenna waited, not too eagerly, in the white wicker rocker. It was a good choice for the green-and-yellow nursery.

"I bought a baby book for our Jonathan," Mom said, carrying the book to Jenna. "Just look at all the different things we can write in your brother's book."

"We? You don't mean *me*, do you?" She looked up at her mother.

"I certainly do. Dad and I . . . and you are going to write in this beautiful book. For the new baby."

Jenna held the book on her lap, hesitating to open the pages. "I wouldn't know what to write," she said softly.

"Well, let me give you an idea." Mom scurried off down the hall to the front of the house, to the master suite.

Jenna had no idea what her mom was searching for. And she didn't exactly care. But she sat quietly, looking around the room at all the new stuff. The cow lamp, the changing table, and the white crib with a green-and-yellow ruffled quilt and tiny sham to match. On the wall, a matching fabric collage was framed in white wicker—to match the rocking chair, Jenna guessed.

Once or twice, she'd poked her head in here since the certified letter had shown up in the mail. But never had she entered the room or allowed herself to get too close to any of the baby furniture.

"Here we are," Mom said as she returned to the nursery, holding a white-and-pink book. "Do you remember this?"

Jenna remembered but hadn't seen *her* baby book for the longest time.

"Look through it, honey. You'll see the wonderful words Daddy and I wrote for you. Notice all the different stages in your infancy, toddlerhood, and up through your preschool years and beyond."

Jenna read with great interest. There were pictures, too. Color snapshots of her parents taking turns holding their tiny daughter—Jenna Lynn Song.

She looked closer, and sure enough! The very same goofy look was on her mother's face in these pictures. The same glazed, almost spaced-out look she'd seen in the car today.

"We fell instantly in love with you," her mom said, kneeling beside the rocking chair. "Look there, how Daddy and I fussed over you."

The picture showed her parents leaning over a crib, on either side, cooing into Jenna's baby face.

"Who took the picture?" she asked.

Mom grinned. "Your father had an automatic camera back then, all set up on a tripod. It was one of his grown-up toys."

Jenna couldn't help herself. She laughed out loud.

"What's so funny?" asked Mom.

"Nothing really . . . and everything, too." She was making at least as much sense as her mom. Or anyone else waiting to adopt a baby, she guessed.

CHAPTER 15

"Guess what I did after I got home from gymnastics yesterday?" Jenna asked Livvy on the phone the next day.

"Beats me."

"C'mon, guess!"

"Honestly, Jenna, I don't know. Just tell me, will ya?"

She heard the impatience in her friend's voice. "Okay, okay. I checked out my old baby book."

"What's the big deal?"

Jenna was quiet. She wasn't sure how to say this. "I'm . . . uh, having second thoughts."

"About what?"

Sighing, Jenna told her. "About being okay with—"

"Your brother's adoption?" Livvy interrupted.

"Uh-huh." She wondered what her friend would say now.

"Well, I think it's about time!" Livvy was laughing. "Are you saying what I think you are?"

"Well, not exactly."

"So . . . are you *still* going to the meet this Saturday?" Livvy asked, her breathing filling up the silence.

"You don't have to ask. You know I'm going." She didn't want to argue this subject anymore. But it was clear Livvy wasn't giving up. Her friend had some weird plan, but it was a waste of time. Jenna was sure of it.

"I've gotta run," Livvy said.

"Yeah, me too."

They hung up, and Jenna hurried to change clothes for the midweek church service.

After church, Uncle Nam motioned to her. He was carrying his baby boy—Jenna's new cousin—showing him off. "You haven't said hello to Kyung yet." Her uncle leaned down so she could have a close-up look.

Jenna peered down into the face of the tiny bundle. "Oh, he's cute," she whispered, touching the tiny cheek with her pointer finger.

"Kyung's *handsome*—the handiwork of God," crowed Uncle Nam.

"You're right," she said.

Unexpectedly, Baby Kyung wrapped his teeny fingers around her own, and her heart did a double salto with a full twist. "How sweet," she whispered, surprised at her reaction.

Uncle Nam was more than a proud father. He was generous, too. "Would you like to hold him?" he asked.

"Uh . . . I better not." Jenna hadn't been one to baby-sit

or take care of little ones through the years. In fact, she had never baby-sat like many of her girlfriends. Every free moment was spent at the gym.

"He won't break," Uncle Nam persisted.

If I hold him, he might, she thought.

But before she could voice her concern, the cuddly young cousin was in her arms. The baby made adorable squeaky sounds, almost happy sounds, Jenna thought. And nearly without thinking, she began to rock him gently.

Why was I so afraid? she wondered. *Babies aren't so bad.*

Just then her aunt came down the aisle. "It's getting late," she said, a denim baby bag slung over her shoulders. "We must head home . . . tuck our baby into his cradle."

Reluctantly, Jenna returned her cousin to his father. "Bye-bye, handsome baby," she said softly.

Uncle Nam nodded, wearing a big smile. "Remember . . . he's God's creation." Then he turned and headed for the foyer area, talking in Korean to his sleeping son, then to his wife.

Jenna's brain buzzed with unexpected thoughts. She sat on the last pew in the sanctuary, thinking about tiny Kyung. Uncle Nam was right. There was something very precious about the baby. Something belonging to God.

The chapel was soon empty of people, except for her parents and one other church member. She could hear sounds of the branches brushing against the trees outside. A white half-moon peeked through one of the stained-glass windows.

Leaning back against the wooden pew, Jenna wondered if the baby boy from Korea would affect her this way. Would she miss holding him the way she missed her new little cousin right now?

She thought more about the idea of a baby brother. And when she tried to picture what he might look like, she started to feel the tiniest shiver of excitement. Until yesterday, sitting in the nursery at home, she'd had no interest in being a big sister to an orphaned infant. But now? She could hardly wait to meet her new brother, Jonathan Song.

Most of all, she wondered how she would tell Coach Kim and Tasya. She'd have to forfeit the meet after all. But how would Coach and Tasya take it? Giving them only three days' notice wasn't very sportsmanlike. Not fair at all. She worried about that. But she knew it was her fault for waiting this long—for disobeying her parents.

Looking into the dear little face of cousin Kyung—God's creation—had touched her. It had begun to change things.

Maybe everything.

CHAPTER 16

Thursday morning, Jenna hurried downstairs to breakfast. She was still wearing her pajamas and bathrobe. "Good morning, everybody," she said, sitting at the kitchen table.

"Well, aren't *you* the cheerful one?" Dad said, putting the paper aside.

Her mother did a double take. "Your hair looks like it woke up on the wrong side of the bed!"

Laughing, Jenna reached her hand up to her head. She felt the hairs sticking out. "Hey, you're right," she said, giggling.

"Maybe this is a new hairstyle," Dad said, reaching for his cup of coffee.

"Could be," she said. "I'll have to see what Livvy thinks."

"By the way, Livvy called here earlier," Mom said. "She

asked if you can meet her at the mall skating rink before school."

Jenna glanced at the wall clock above the sink. "If I hurry, maybe I can."

"I'll drive you, if that helps," offered Dad.

"Thanks." She wondered what her best friend was up to.

Quickly, she went upstairs to shower and dress. Before heading to her room, she crept away to the yellow-and-green nursery at the end of the hall. Standing beside the crib, she looked down. She touched the ruffled crib sham and quilted coverlet. It was easy to imagine a baby sleeping there. A baby as adorable as her very own cousin.

On the way to the rink, Jenna asked her dad about the Saturday plans. "What time is the appointment at the adoption agency?" she asked.

"Eleven o'clock sharp," he replied without glancing her way. "Why do you ask?"

She didn't tell him why. Not yet. "I just wondered" was all she said. She figured they'd leave for Denver around seven-thirty. Because, knowing her parents, they'd want to be as prompt as possible.

"Your mother and I expect that you already made arrangements with Coach Kim . . . to inform the alternate." He pulled up to the curb.

"Don't worry, Dad," she said before getting out.

He stopped the car near the entrance to the mini shopping center. "I'm not worried, Jenna, and you mustn't be, either. Trust the Lord for His plan for your future. For our family's, too."

He seemed almost ready to step behind a pulpit. For as long as she remembered, her dad was always eager to get a word in for God. "Thanks for the ride," she said, opening the door.

"Any time!" He smiled and waved.

Jenna watched him pull away from the curb. "What a really cool father," she whispered before heading into the mall to find Livvy.

The skating rink was situated in the center of the small emporium. There were live trees decorated with giant red bows and white lights for the holidays. Quaint benches scattered the area.

Tired of lugging her gym bag, Jenna sat on one of the benches and waited for Livvy to finish up her session. There were several other advanced skaters on the ice. Two ice dancers caught her eye. They looked like twins—a boy and girl about Jenna's age.

Who are they? she wondered, her eyes glued to the incredible blond twosome.

Livvy soon spotted her and motioned for her to come to the edge of the rink. "Your mom must've told you I called," she said, catching her breath.

"Yep, that's why I'm here. What's up?"

Glancing over her shoulder, Livvy said, "See those ice dancers?"

"How could I miss them? I can't take my eyes off them . . . especially the boy." Jenna smothered a giggle. "Who are they?"

"Heather and Kevin Bock. And they're really super skaters."

"I noticed." Jenna watched the pair circle past. "They must be twins—they look so much alike."

"They're twenty months apart. Best friends, too!" Livvy turned and watched them for a moment.

"I've never seen them at school," Jenna said.

"That's because they're homeschooled."

"Really?" Jenna was dying to meet them. Especially Kevin. "So when are you gonna introduce me?"

"As soon as they take their break," Livvy said, grinning. "I really wanted you to meet Heather because she's starting ballet after Christmas."

"With *us*?"

Livvy nodded, facing her now. "And there's another reason why I want you to meet Heather and Kevin." Her merry face had turned serious.

"Why?" asked Jenna.

"They have a younger brother and sister . . . both adopted."

Jenna should have known. "That's interesting," she said, playing along.

"Wait here," Livvy said, skating off toward center ice.

Jenna watched as Livvy chatted with the Bock kids.

Being new to the mountain town, she was glad to meet more young athletes. Kids with similar goals ... and kids with adopted siblings. She wondered how many *more* adopted people she was going to meet in one week!

Jenna went looking for Coach Kim as soon as she arrived at the gym. It was one of her off days, so she knew he wouldn't be expecting to see her.

She found him positioning heavy safety mats under and around the balance beam. "Jenna, what a nice surprise!" His big voice bounced across the gym.

"Uh, excuse me, Coach." She wished she could hide under the largest floor mat. "I need to talk to you."

His usually jovial face turned to a frown. "Is something wrong?"

"No . . . actually, everything's *right*." Suddenly, she felt more confident. "I should've told you this two weeks ago. I'm sorry I waited so long." She explained about the baby her parents were going to adopt. That she would have to miss the meet and go to Denver instead. "I haven't been much of a team member," she confessed. "You always say we're a family here at AAG—that we work together. But I haven't acted like a part of this family."

Coach Kim's face broke into a big smile. "On the contrary, Jenna. What you're doing with your parents is far more important than any gymnastics meet. You mustn't forget that. Only the best kind of person would do what you're doing." He touched her head gently. "You are one of those people, Jenna. You will make the new baby a very good sister."

She thought she might cry. "I hope the team won't hate me for this . . . for backing out so late."

He put his finger to her lips. "Hate never built a strong family . . . or a team. Nobody's going to say a word about this. I promise you."

She hugged him and said good-bye, then hurried outside. On the long walk home, she thought of Cassie and Lara and the others. How would the All-Around Team score without her? How would the competition play out? Who would they pick for the alternate?

Her heart sank as she thought again of missing out. But she knew she'd made the right choice. It was the best choice for her family—and for her new brother.

When she arrived home, her mother met her at the door. "Livvy's on the phone. She sounds very excited."

Jenna rushed into the house and picked up the living room phone. "Livvy? Hi, what's up?"

"I've been thinking."

"Better be careful, that could be dangerous," she said, laughing.

"No, seriously. Let's start a club. For girls only."

"With *two* members?"

"Well, no. Actually, I was thinking about including Heather Bock. If it's all right with you," Livvy said. "What do you think?"

"Of the club or Heather?"

"Both."

Jenna really liked the idea. "Sure, why not? Heather's really cool. What's *she* think of your idea?"

"I haven't said anything because I wanted to talk to my best friend about it first." Livvy was laughing. "You *are* my best friend, you know!"

"Sounds like we might be expanding to three." She wondered how long it would take to get to know Heather Bock. *Really* know her the way she and Livvy knew each other.

"When should we have our first club meeting?" Livvy asked.

Jenna was ready now! "How about right away?"

"You're kidding."

Jenna chuckled. "Come over in a half hour. Let's start by practicing our ballet stretches and moves at the barre in my bedroom. Isn't my attic room the perfect place?"

Livvy agreed. "I'll call Heather. See ya!"

Jenna hung up the phone and went searching for her mom. "We've got company coming . . . Livvy and Heather. Hope it's all right with you." She told her mother all about Livvy's club idea. And about Heather and Kevin.

Mom's face brightened as she sat at the kitchen table. "Sounds like fun."

"We won't bother you if we work out in my room, will we?"

"That's fine," Mom said. "And when you're finished with your meeting, maybe the girls can stay and help us put up the Christmas tree."

Jenna was pleased. Mom was bending over backward to be agreeable. "I'm getting to be a pro at decorating trees," she said.

"Oh?"

She described how she and Lara had put up the little tree at the gym. "And this afternoon, I talked to Coach Kim . . . finally. Everything's set. I'll miss this one meet, but he understood." Saying the words brought a twinge of pain, but Jenna didn't regret her decision.

"*I* talked to Coach Kim today, too," her mother said. "What a fine coach you have."

"We all knew he was from the start."

Mom smiled knowingly. "It's even more obvious to me now."

Jenna didn't pry. She didn't ask her mom about the conversation with Coach Kim. "I'm sorry for dragging my feet about canceling the meet," she said. "I really wanted to go."

"I know, honey. It was a difficult thing for you to do. I'm very proud of you. Both Dad and I are."

Jenna hugged her mom and held on tight. "I can't wait to meet our baby," she said, pulling away at last. "And I mean that."

"Would you like a sneak preview?" Mom asked, getting

up and heading for the dining room.

"What do you mean?" She followed Mom to the buffet.

There, between two china candleholders, was a tiny face with the cutest nose and the sweetest eyes.

Mom picked up the framed picture. "This is Jonathan. The photo came in the mail today."

"And you framed it already?" Jenna gazed at the adorable face.

"I couldn't help myself," Mom said.

"I think I know how you feel," Jenna replied.

Jenna chose one of her favorite classical CDs—*Peer Gynt Suite*. "Wait'll you hear this," she said as the Girls Only club members prepared to do their ballet warm-ups.

"Heather's a classical music nut, too," Livvy said, smiling. "Just like me."

The blond ice dancer nodded. She wore a pale blue jogging outfit that brought out the blue of her eyes. "I like all different kinds of music," she said. "Music brings out the zip and pizzazz in me . . . in my brother, too. We always talk over what music we like best for our ice-dancing routines."

Jenna wondered what it would be like to have a partnership with an older brother. "Do you ever blame Kevin for flubs or getting marked down at competitions?" she asked.

Heather shook her head. "No . . . never. We've worked as a team since I was in second grade and Kevin in third."

"That long? Wow," Jenna said. "So you really know what to expect from each other?"

"Always." Heather went to sit next to Livvy on the floor, under the barre. "This is really some special place," she said, glancing around the room.

"Thanks," Jenna said. "You should've seen it before we put in the new carpet and the wallpaper. It was such a mess."

Livvy nodded. "It sure was. But then, so was the old Victorian house my dad bought on Main Street. Remodeling is the thing—for ancient houses, at least."

The girls chatted about their homes, parents, and school. Heather showed off a wallet picture of her grade-school-age adopted brother and sister. "It's just like they were born into the family—no difference," she said.

Jenna wondered how that could be. She guessed she'd find out sooner or later.

The girls began discussing the club name. "Is *Girls Only* okay with you two?" Livvy asked.

Jenna pulled up her knees, leaning her chin on them. "I don't know about either of you, but I think it's a really cool name for our club," she said. "It's got a lot of class."

"Yeah, and the initials spell *GO*—which describes each of us exactly," Livvy said.

Heather nodded. "Because we're always so active, right?"

The girls agreed, grinning at each other.

Jenna went to her desk and changed the CD. "Who's ready for some Christmas tunes?" she asked.

Livvy and Heather definitely were. And within seconds, the strains of "Greensleeves" floated through the attic room. "Hey, let's work up a ballet routine to this!" Heather said, getting up and twirling on her toes.

"Super!" Livvy said, mimicking Heather.

Jenna liked the idea but stopped to look out one of the dormer windows near her desk. A light snow had begun to fall again, just since Livvy and Heather had arrived. The tops of the neighbors' houses were already dusted white.

She didn't tell Livvy or Heather that her thoughts were on the All-Around Team. *Her* team was going to Colorado Springs without their captain!

Putting on a smile, Jenna did her best to count off the dance steps. She followed Heather's lead. With every move, she focused on *GO!*—a cool club for a super threesome.

Thursday, December 3
Dear Diary,

I can't believe it's almost Saturday! Mom's got everything ready for the baby—diapers, bottles, blankets, clothes, and the tiniest bibs. Dad's still trying out middle names to go with Jonathan.

Me? I'm getting used to the idea of sharing my parents with somebody else. Somebody new!

Heather Bock's really cool. Livvy and I had a great time getting better acquainted with her. (She doesn't know it, but we both think her brother Kevin is VERY cute!)

Our first official GO! club activity was to memorize a ballet routine—which Heather helped create. We're really good at it, for only just working it up. Maybe we can perform it during Christmas—for our parents.

Livvy and Heather stayed to help decorate our liv-

ing room tree—just like Mom had hoped. We all got along so well together. (Even Dad was impressed with Heather's good attitude and helpful nature. He says there's something special about homeschooled kids!)

The girls think the nursery is darling. Livvy said it was "super sweet." Heather doesn't have any favorite word to describe things. At least, I haven't noticed one yet.

Tomorrow Mom and I are going to Uncle Nam's to see baby Kyung again. Mom wants to ask more questions about baby care—Korean style. I know it's because she wants to be the best mother for Jonathan. But knowing my mom, she'll do just fine. After all, look how I'm turning out!

I finally heard Livvy's "plan" for my Saturday. Her uncle's got a private pilot's license, from what she said. She had this crazy idea that if I could work things out, I could go with the team to the meet at the Olympic Training Center. Her Chicago uncle would fly in and take me to Denver just in time to meet my parents and the baby.

It was an interesting thought while it lasted. . . .

CHAPTER 19

Early Saturday morning, Jenna stared up at the Olympic rings flag above her computer desk. "Go, team," she said, stretching in her bed. "Hit everything at the meet. Do it for me."

Heading down the hall, she turned on the shower and let the water run. She peered into the mirror over the sink. A sleepy-eyed, All-Around Team captain in a pink-flannel nightgown stared back at her. A girl with high goals and lofty dreams.

She drank a glass of water. Looking in the mirror again, she saw a Korean pastor's daughter. An only child about to become a sister.

The ride to Denver seemed never-ending. Dad rehearsed

a hundred different middle names for the baby. Mom read aloud from a baby-care book.

Jenna had to smile at her parents' approach to all of this. "You act like you've never done this before," she said.

Mom looked back over the front seat at her. "In case you've forgotten, it's been eleven years since we've had a baby in the house."

"It'll come back quickly," Dad said, offering Mom a reassuring smile. "You're a natural with little ones, dear."

The comment seemed to help. Mom shrugged her shoulders and returned to her reading.

Jenna stared out the car window, watching the mountains blur past. *This is my first day as a sister*, she thought, deciding to be the best one Jonathan could possibly have. More than that, she wanted to make her parents glad they'd given birth to her.

"I think I'm ready to write in the baby book," she spoke up. "Did you bring it along?"

Her mom pointed to a canvas bag next to Jenna on the backseat. "It's in that bag right there."

Opening the bag, Jenna looked inside. Her pink leotard, palm protectors, wrist guards, and beam slippers were in the bag, too. "I wondered where these were," she said, reaching for the baby book instead.

Mom stopped reading. "There's a page close to the front," she said. "You'll see the heading—*The Day You Came To Live With Us*."

Jenna scanned the baby book. She hadn't realized that it was a book for adopted children. Totally different from the one her mother had kept for her.

She read the words her parents had written, wondering how her brother would feel reading them, too, when he was much older. Finding a pen in her purse, she clicked it on and began to write.

> *To my brother, Jonathan:*
> *You don't know me yet, but I know something about you. Your eyes and your cute little face in our first picture of you made me feel happy all over. I hope you like being a member of our "team."*
> > *Love,*
> > *Your big sister, Jenna*

She read through the entire book, understanding how each page related to an adopted child. By the time she was finished, they were coming into the busy outskirts of the big city of Denver.

Mom double-checked the map and gave Dad directions to the adoption agency. Jenna felt the first butterflies in her stomach. She thought about Cassie—how proud she was to be adopted. And Heather's wallet picture of her little brother and sister. So many happy "adoptive" families . . .

At least five different times, Jenna checked to make sure tiny Jonathan was snug and secure in his infant car seat next to her. She wished she could hold him all the way back to Alpine Lake, but he was much safer where he was.

"Jonathan Bryan is the cutest baby on earth," Jenna said, using the middle name her parents had finally chosen.

She settled back in the seat, staring at him. Jonathan was as olive-skinned as she was but with darker hair. His fingers and hands were perfectly formed, and when he sighed, she knew she wanted to protect him forever.

"How fast do babies grow?" she asked, leaning forward.

"Oh, he'll be walking in six or seven months from now," her mom said.

"How old was I when I took my first steps?" she asked.

Dad chuckled. "You were an early one, Jenna. We always knew we had a gymnast in the family."

"Tell me again." She'd heard the story many times but wanted to hear it again. Just for fun.

"Well, you liked to somersault and balance your feet on anything that resembled a straight line," Mom said.

"And always with your arms out and your head tilted up," Dad said. "You were moving constantly."

Jenna watched her sleeping four-month-old brother. *Will Jonathan be a gymnast, too?* she wondered.

Her mother was rattling the map in the front seat. But Jenna noticed that the sound didn't startle her brother at all. "Looks like he's a sound sleeper."

Mom turned around. "The caseworker said he sleeps straight through five hours at night."

"And then he wants to be fed, right?" she said.

Her dad glanced over at her mom. "We'll take turns getting up with him," he offered, reaching his arm around Mom.

"I'll help, too," Jenna said.

"But gymnasts need a full night of sleep," Mom said,

handing the map back to her. "Here, see if you can find the turnoff for Interstate 25."

"What for?" she asked, opening the map.

"We need to help Dad find the way to Colorado Springs," said her mother.

Her mom's words didn't quite register in her brain, but she started looking for the highway. Suddenly, she realized what Mom had said. "Why are we going to Colorado Springs?" she asked, her heart thumping hard.

Mom was smiling the most curious smile. "You have a gymnastics meet to attend this afternoon," she said.

"I *what*?" Jenna could hardly believe her ears.

Dad was nodding his head and looking at her in his rear-view mirror. "Coach Kim said if we could get you to the Olympic Training Center by two o'clock, you could compete with the team."

"Oh, you're kidding! This is so cool!" And she leaned over and whispered to the baby, "You're going to your first gymnastics competition, Jonathan Bryan Song."

Then she leaned back against the seat and began psyching herself up for competition. She thought through each of her routines. When she came to the floor routines in her mind, she visualized a perfect aerial cartwheel. She'd do her very best to hit everything. For the team . . . and for baby Jonathan.

CHAPTER 20

"Jenna, you're here!" Cassie said, clapping and smiling.

All the girls circled her, calling out encouragement to each other and to Jenna.

"Where were you?" Cassie asked. "Why didn't you ride along with the team?"

"It's a long story . . . but a very cool one," she said.

Cassie frowned. "I have no idea what you're talking about."

"Don't worry, I'll tell you later." She almost said *I'll show you* but didn't want to draw the focus off the competition. After the meet, there'd be plenty of time for introductions to her baby brother.

Coach Kim and Tasya helped the girls pep up with words like "We can do it!" and "We're going to hit everything . . . everything!"

The atmosphere was electric. Cassie was right, the place

was totally amazing and buzzing with the crowd and the competitors.

Jenna had plenty of time for some short warm-ups with the rest of the team. She felt so good, like the confidence might burst right out of her.

"I feel so ready for this," she said to Cassie. "How are you doing?"

A smile broke over Cassie's face. "I thought I wanted to do other things," she said softly. "Things that I was maybe kind of good at without having to work so hard . . . you know, the way we do in gymnastics. But I've made a decision."

"You're staying in?" asked Jenna, reaching to hug Cassie. "You're not quitting, are you?"

"Things that come easy aren't worth doing, are they?" Cassie replied, her eyes glistening.

"Yes!" shouted Jenna.

The girls danced around, hugging and laughing. "I'm going to nail every single routine today," Cassie said. "I promised myself."

"Me too," Jenna said. She glanced up in the stands and saw her dad waving a banner. On the bench sat her mom, holding Jonathan. Tears threatened to spill over, but Jenna waved at the three of them instead. "I love you," she whispered.

The girls were chanting behind her. "Hit it . . . hit it. . . ." Over and over they said the words, until there was so much energy around them, Jenna was dying to get started. They all were.

Finally the All-Around Team from Alpine Aerials Gymnastics marched into the arena. Jenna was first in the line of eight girls because they were arranged in stairsteps—shortest to tallest. Each girl was so pumped up and ready.

They warmed up some more and then started the competition on the uneven parallel bars. Jenna was up third, right after Cassie and Lara. She prayed silently before the judges gave her the green light to begin. All three girls nailed one routine after another. So did the rest of the team.

The vault was next, followed by the balance beam. Jenna remembered everything Coach Kim and Tasya had told her. She flew through her routines, hitting every single one!

They went to the floor mats, trailing another team from Grand Junction, Colorado. But that gave Jenna and the others all the more courage to do their best.

"Only the best . . ."

She could hear her mother's words in her ears as she saluted the judges. Jenna focused on her tumbling run, took a deep breath, and hit every element with complete confidence. Even the aerial cartwheel—crisp and clean!

The crowd was cheering as she raised her hands high over her head. *Yes! I did it. I did it. . . .*

When her score—9.820—flashed on the scoreboard, she thought she heard her parents cheering. She strained her ears to sort out the sounds, and she was sure now. Because their shouts of glee were in Korean.

And then she heard a baby's cry. Jonathan? Was her baby brother "cheering" for her, too? In his own unique way, she knew he was.

It was one of the best days of her life.

That night, after she helped her mom tuck Jonathan into his crib, she sat down to her computer. She keyed in the email address for Dominique Moceanu and began her message.

> Hi again, Domi,
>
> I had my first meet at OTC in Colorado Springs. You said I'd love it, and I did.
>
> Guess what! My parents adopted a baby boy today. Actually, the adoption will be finalized several months from now. But I thought you'd enjoy this, especially since your little sister is eight years younger than you are.
>
> My new brother's name is Jonathan Bryan. Does that sound like the name of a famous gymnast???
>
> I'm so excited about how well our team did today. We aren't Elite gymnasts yet, but we're on our way. Our team placed fifth in the state. Not bad for small-town girls!
>
> I feel so pepped up tonight. I wish I could send an email to Shannon Miller and Amy Chow, too. Their performances at the Olympics, along with yours, gave me the heart to keep trying to HIT EVERYTHING in all my workouts and competitions.
>
> Thanks for your friendship, Domi. I hope you make it to the 2000 Olympics.
>
> > Bye for now,
> > Jenna Song

She read her message quickly before sending it, then

called for Sasha. "Come here, little girl. I haven't seen you all day," she said, coaxing the drowsy feline onto the bed. "You're not the only baby around here anymore. You're gonna share my attention with a real baby. How do you like that?"

Sasha opened her eyes, then blinked slowly and was soon snoozing again.

"Sweet dreams," Jenna whispered and turned out the light.

She thanked God for working things out for her and her family and for the team. Her mother came in and tucked her in for the night.

"Thanks for everything, Mom," she said. "You're the best."

"Well, I don't know about that, but it's nice of you to say it." And she sat on the edge of the bed and kissed Jenna's forehead.

After her mom left, Jenna could see the dim hall light through the crack under her bedroom door. Tempted to get up and sneak to the nursery, she lay still, thinking about the day. Her parents had arranged for her to attend the meet. She still could hardly believe it. What a surprise!

If she were to think of the key words for the day's events, she would have to start by saying, "baby brother" and end with "just too cool."

CHAPTER 21

Girls Only—the club—met again on Monday afternoon. Jenna, Livvy, and Heather rehearsed their ballet routine for their Christmas show. They listened to other CDs, too, deciding on additional music.

Later, while sipping apple juice, Jenna told the girls about the incredible gymnastics meet. Then she took them into the nursery, and they each held her brother. "I got what I wanted for Christmas already," she said, stroking Jonathan's little fist.

"Hey, you're right," Livvy said, getting her face up close to the baby's. "Not fair. Santa came early to your house."

They laughed at that, but Jenna knew better. God had brought this baby here. And into her own heart.

Livvy handed the bundle back to Jenna. "I almost forgot to tell you what I heard about Chris and Jamey," she said with a strange look on her face.

"Do we *have* to talk about them at a time like this?" Jenna asked, staring down into her brother's face.

Livvy continued. "The principal gave them a very interesting assignment."

"For a punishment?" asked Jenna, surprised to hear it.

"They have to do a big research paper on Korea . . . all about the geography, capital, population, history. The works."

"You're kidding," she said, wondering if the boys would focus in on the people and their unique looks. The way they had on her these miserable weeks.

"And get this," Livvy said, her face glowing. "They're talking about visiting your father's church on Sunday."

"Are you sure?" Jenna asked, laying the baby down in the crib.

Livvy was giggling now. "Chris says he wants to interview a Korean pastor. He thinks he'll get extra credit for it or something."

"Well, if he interviews my dad, he could end up talking to God, too. You know how my dad is," Jenna said, feeling better about the whole thing.

Livvy nodded. "Sounds like the assignment might not be such a bad thing for them, after all."

"God works things out for good," Jenna said, remembering the Scripture.

"Yeah, in more ways than one, right?" said Livvy.

Heather was smiling, too.

Jenna and the girls tiptoed out of the nursery. She was excited about the future. Her future as a gymnast—and as a sister.

Don't miss GIRLS ONLY *(GO!)* #3

A Perfect Match

Heather and Kevin Bock, sister/brother ice dancers, are among the top competitors for the Summer Ice Spectacular trophy. But Heather confides to Livvy Hudson and Jenna Song, her *Girls Only* club member friends, that she wants to switch to figure skating. Livvy and Jenna are shocked; after all, the dynamic duo have been a pair since grade school. Why would Heather want to throw away years of training?

Meanwhile, Kevin wastes no time looking for a new partner. A talented figure skater catches his eye—on and off the ice—and Kevin wants to audition her to replace Heather.

After a solid week of training with a figure-skating coach, Heather has second thoughts. Is it too late to return to ice dancing? Will Kevin agree to take her back? Or are her Olympic dreams slipping away?

Also by Beverly Lewis

PICTURE BOOK

Cows in the House

THE CUL-DE-SAC KIDS
Children's Fiction

The Double Dabble Surprise	*The Mudhole Mystery*
The Chicken Pox Panic	*Fiddlesticks*
The Crazy Christmas Angel Mystery	*The Crabby Cat Caper*
No Grown-ups Allowed	*Tarantula Toes*
Frog Power	*Green Gravy*
The Mystery of Case D. Luc	*Backyard Bandit Mystery*
The Stinky Sneakers Mystery	*Tree House Trouble*
Pickle Pizza	*The Creepy Sleep-Over*
Mailbox Mania	*The Great TV Turn-Off*

SUMMERHILL SECRETS
Youth Fiction

Whispers Down the Lane	*A Cry in the Dark*
Secret in the Willows	*House of Secrets*
Catch a Falling Star	*Echoes in the Wind*
Night of the Fireflies	*Hide Behind the Moon*

HOLLY'S HEART SERIES
Youth Fiction

Holly's First Love	*Straight-A Teacher*
Secret Summer Dreams	*The "No-Guys" Pact*
Sealed With a Kiss	*Little White Lies*
The Trouble With Weddings	*Freshmen Frenzy*
California Christmas	*Mystery Letters*
Second-Best Friend	*Eight Is Enough*
Good-bye, Dressel Hills	*It's a Girl Thing*

THE HERITAGE OF LANCASTER COUNTY
Adult Fiction

The Shunning	*The Confession*
The Reckoning	

GIFT BOOK

The Sunroom

Series for Middle Graders* From BHP

ADVENTURES DOWN UNDER · by Robert Elmer
When Patrick McWaid's father is unjustly sent to Australia as a prisoner in 1867, the rest of the family follows, uncovering action-packed mystery along the way.

ADVENTURES OF THE NORTHWOODS · by Lois Walfrid Johnson
Kate O'Connell and her stepbrother Anders encounter mystery and adventure in northwest Wisconsin near the turn of the century.

AN AMERICAN ADVENTURE SERIES · by Lee Roddy
Hildy Corrigan and her family must overcome danger and hardship during the Great Depression as they search for a "forever home."

BLOODHOUNDS, INC. · by Bill Myers
Hilarious, hair-raising suspense follows brother-and-sister detectives Sean and Melissa Hunter in these madcap mysteries with a message.

GIRLS ONLY! · by Beverly Lewis
Four talented young athletes become fast friends as together they pursue their Olympic dreams.

JOURNEYS TO FAYRAH · by Bill Myers
Join Denise, Nathan, and Josh on amazing journeys as they discover the wonders and lessons of the mystical Kingdom of Fayrah.

MANDIE BOOKS · by Lois Gladys Leppard
With over four million sold, the turn-of-the-century adventures of Mandie and her many friends will keep readers eager for more.

THE RIVERBOAT ADVENTURES · by Lois Walfrid Johnson
Libby Norstad and her friend Caleb face the challenges and risks of working with the Underground Railroad during the mid–1800s.

TRAILBLAZER BOOKS · by Dave and Neta Jackson
Follow the exciting lives of real-life Christian heroes through the eyes of child characters as they share their faith with others around the world.

THE TWELVE CANDLES CLUB · by Elaine L. Schulte
When four twelve-year-old girls set up a business of odd jobs and baby-sitting, they uncover wacky adventures and hilarious surprises.

THE YOUNG UNDERGROUND · by Robert Elmer
Peter and Elise Andersen's plots to protect their friends and themselves from Nazi soldiers in World War II Denmark guarantee fast-paced action and suspenseful reads.

*(ages 8–13)